A Place for Everyone

by Barbara Resch
English text by Philomena Korbutt

atomium books

Ephie and Josephine were very good friends. They lived in a lush green jungle — a perfect place for two elephants.

But Ephie wasn't happy there. Her big, beautiful, pink ears always made her feel so different from everyone else. She longed to be more like her friend Josephine, who was small, grey, and happy about herself.

"I don't fit in here," Ephie sighed one day.

"Why?" asked Josephine. "Everyone loves looking through your ears! They make the world look so rosy pink and cheerful."

"That doesn't matter to me — I just can't stay here any longer," Ephie responded sadly.

"Then let's go and find a place where you can be happy," said her little friend.

That very evening, as the sun was setting,
they left the jungle and started their search.
A brightly colored bird decided to join them.

Their search led them to many new and interesting places. They enjoyed each discovery they made — especially the clear, blue lake where they stopped to play.

"Look I can make my own shower!" exclaimed Ephie, splashing happily.

Josephine didn't answer. She was almost completely underwater.

"Josephine can't hear you," laughed the bird. "She's pretending to be a spouting fountain."

Later, on the edge of a desert, they met a family of lions, relaxing in the shade of a tree. The lions had never seen an elephant with pink ears before.

The little cubs ran up to take a closer look at Ephie's ears. The cubs were so excited when they looked through them and saw the world turn rosy pink!

But the mother lioness felt uneasy at seeing such strange ears and asked her cubs to come back.

This made Ephie feel sadder than ever, so she and Josephine decided not to stay.

Their next discovery was a cove filled with pink flamingos.

"Maybe I'll fit in here," said Ephie. "Just look at the beautiful pink wings on these birds! Don't they remind you of me?"

"But can you fly?" asked Josephine.

"I suppose I could give it a try," said Ephie courageously.

Ephie began to flap her ears.
Slowly they lifted her off the ground.

Josephine grabbed Ephie's tail
and held on tight. They were flying!

But Ephie couldn't fly as quickly as the flamingos,
and they soon disappeared ahead of her.
Flying was very tiring. Ephie decided
to land in the desert.

They walked and walked through the hot yellow sands.
Josephine's little legs couldn't carry her any further.
Ephie picked her up and they continued on their journey.

   "This desert looks like it goes on forever," Ephie sighed.
Her legs were getting tired too.

   "Not much further," encouraged the little bird.
"I see an oasis up ahead."

The oasis was filled with all sorts of different creatures.

But no one else looked like Ephie,
and again she felt uncomfortable.

So the friends trudged on deeper into the desert.
It was a very quiet place. The only sound
that could be heard was the soft whisper of the wind.

The little bird flew ahead of them and spotted
a small patch of green on the horizon.
He hurried back to tell the two very tired elephants.

The green at the edge of the desert turned out
to be a small forest. When they got closer,
they saw flashes of pink amid the trees.

"Maybe the flamingos are waiting for us,"
shouted Josephine.

"No!" exclaimed Ephie.
"Those aren't flamingos — they're elephants!
Elephants with pink ears!"

Ephie was so excited!
She rushed into the forest to greet them.
Her small friend stood back and watched.

Ephie brought Josephine over to the group.

"This is my good friend," she said proudly.

"But she has grey ears," all the elephants said together. "We're not sure if we can like an elephant who looks so different."

Now it was Josephine who felt out of place.
But she was determined not to give up easily.
She could tell that Ephie was happy here.
What could she do to show the forest elephants
that they *could* like her?

"I have lots of stories I can tell you," Josephine said
shyly. "Would you like to hear some of them?"

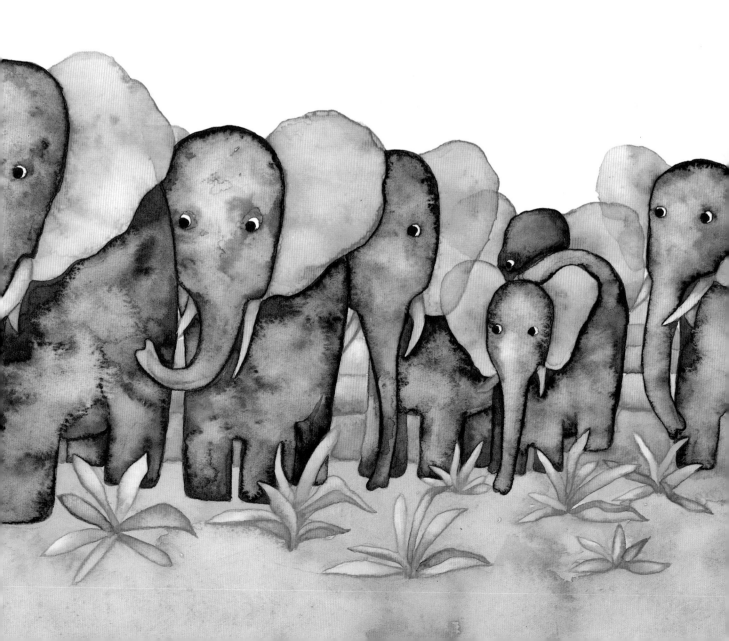

All the elephants agreed to listen, so Josephine began.
She started with a story about pink flamingos flying.
Then she told them about playing in the clean,
refreshing lake and how it felt to travel through
the endlessly silent desert.

She even told them stories about how
it felt to look different.

Her stories lasted long into the night — but everyone was still listening.

Josephine described everything so beautifully that they felt as if they were living inside her stories.

The oldest elephant spoke up. "You have a real gift for telling stories."

Josephine looked around and saw everyone nodding their head in agreement.

All the pink-eared elephants begged Josephine to stay and live with them.

Then Ephie realized what her little friend had known all along. You don't have to look the same to fit in!

Josephine looked at Ephie and their eyes twinkled.
Yes, they would love to stay, they agreed.

Then Josephine told another story. It was about a place
where all the elephants had green ears . . . all except one.

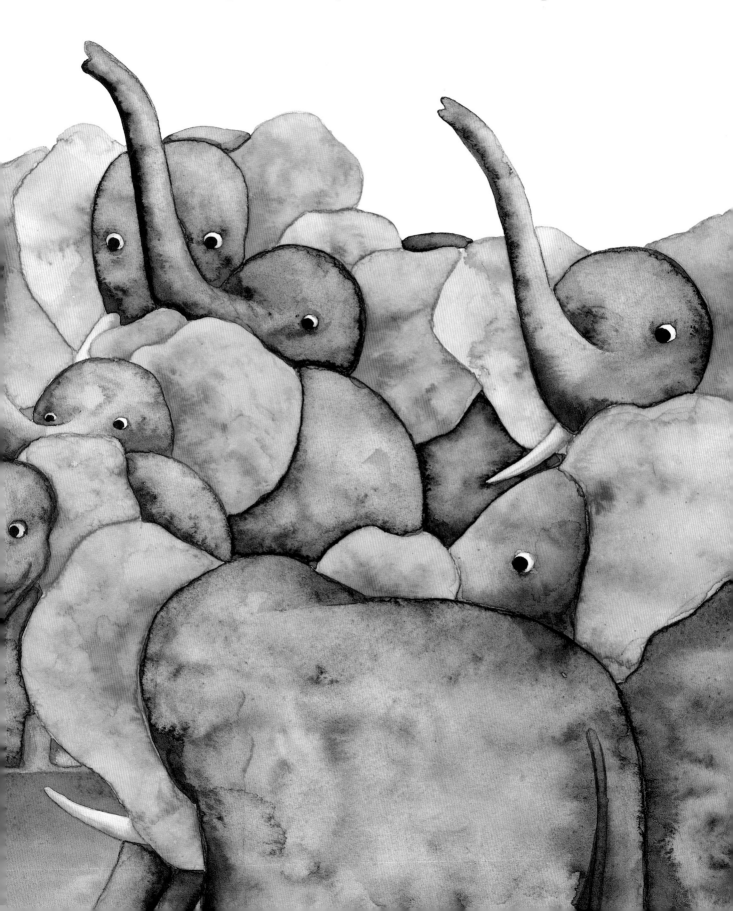

First published in the United States 1990 by

Atomium Books Inc.
Suite 300
1013 Centre Road
Wilmington, DE 19805.

First edition published in German, by Verlag Jungbrunnen,
Vienna - Munich, 1988 under the title "Anderswo ist überall."
Original German text by Alfred Jungraithmayr.
Copyright © Verlag Jungbrunnen 1988.
English translation copyright © Atomium Books 1990.

Printed and bound in Belgium
by Color Print Graphix, Antwerp.
First U.S. Edition
ISBN 1-56182-022-9
2 4 6 8 10 9 7 5 3 1